W9-BCB-343

The Child's World®

Published in the United States of America by The Child's World®
1980 Lookout Drive • Mankato, MN 56003-1705
800-599-READ • www.childsworld.com

ACKNOWLEDGMENTS
The Child's World®: Mary Berendes, Publishing Director
The Design Lab: Kathleen Petelinsek, Design and Page Production
Literacy Consultants: Cecilia Minden, PhD, and Joanne Meier, PhD

LIBRARY OF CONGRESS
CATALOGING-IN-PUBLICATION DATA
Moncure, Jane Belk.
  My "q" sound box / by Jane Belk Moncure ;
illustrated by Rebecca Thornburgh.
    p. cm. — (Sound box books)
  Summary: "Little q has an adventure with items beginning with
her letter's sound, such as quilts, quail, quarters, and a quarrel-
ing queen."—Provided by publisher.
  ISBN 978-1-60253-157-4 (library bound : alk. paper)
  [1. Alphabet.] I. Thornburgh, Rebecca McKillip, ill. II. Title.
III. Series.
  PZ7.M739Myq 2009
  [E]–dc22   2008033173

A NOTE TO PARENTS AND EDUCATORS:

Magic moon machines and five fat frogs are just a few of the fun things you can share with children by reading books with them. Reading aloud helps children in so many ways! It introduces them to new words, motivates them to develop their own reading skills, and expands their attention span and listening abilities. So it's important to find time each day to share a book or two . . . or three!

As you read with young children, you can help develop their understanding of how print works by talking about the parts of the book—the cover, the title, the illustrations, and the words that tell the story. As you read, use your finger to point to each word, modeling a gentle sweep from left to right.

Simple word games help develop important prereading skills, including an understanding of rhyme and alliteration (when words share the same beginning sound, such as "six" and "sand"). Try playing with words from a book you've just shared: "What other words start with the same sound as moon?" "Cat and hat, do those words rhyme?" The possibilities are endless—and so are the rewards!

My "q" Sound Box®

WRITTEN BY JANE BELK MONCURE

ILLUSTRATED BY REBECCA THORNBURGH

Little **a** had a box. "I will find things that begin with my **q** sound," she said. "I will put them into my sound box."

Little  found quilts. . .

. . . quite a lot of quilts! Two quails

watched her quietly.

Little  folded the quilts. She filled her box with quilts.

There was one quilt left. Little
wrapped the quilt around herself.

"I can be a  queen," she said.

Just then, Little 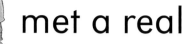 met a real

 queen.

"If you want to look like a real  queen, you must have a crown," said the  queen.

So Little  found some quarters. . .

quite a lot of quarters! She

counted her quarters. How

many did she have?

Little  took the quarters to the store. Little bought a crown. The two queens played until they were quite hungry.

Little 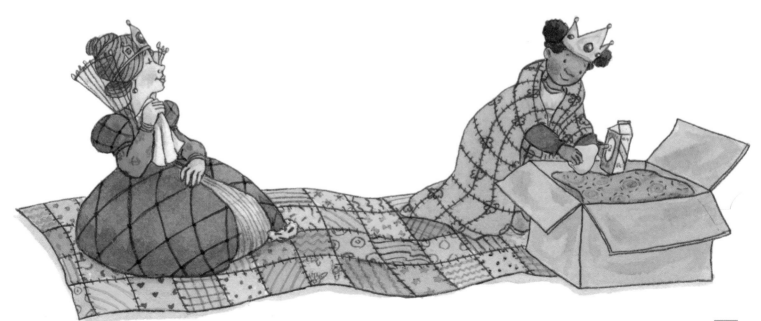 found a quart of milk and some quince. Then she and the queen ate lunch. Little put what was left into the box.

Then Little  said, "It is late!

It is time to go to bed."

"No, no," said the  queen.

"A real 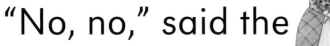 queen must have a

 queen's bed."

Little 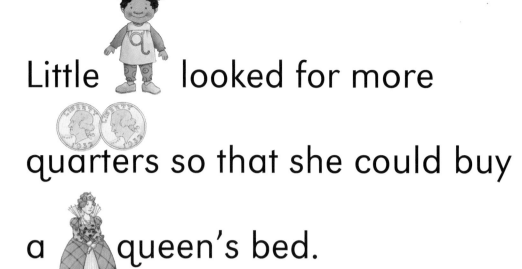 looked for more

quarters so that she could buy

a queen's bed.

She looked and looked. But she could not find any more quarters.

Then Little  saw her box with

all the quilts inside.

"I will turn my box into a queen's bed," she said.

Little  put a quilt on top of the box. "Now we can go to bed," she said. She jumped into the box.

"No! No! No!" said the real  queen.

They quarreled and quarreled

until quarter past nine.

Then the real  queen was so

tired of quarreling that she quit!

She got into the box with Little .

They pulled up the quilt and

went to sleep.

Little 's Word List

quail

quarter

quilt

quart

queen

quince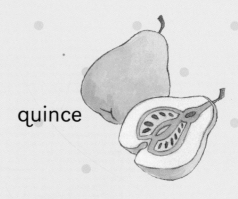

Other Words with Little

Quaker

quartz

quiz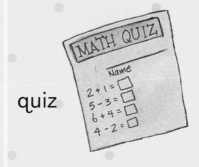

quarterback

quills

quotation marks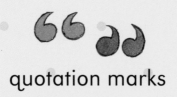

quartet

quintuplets

More to Do!

Little  and the queen had a good night's sleep under their quilt. You can make your own paper quilt!

Q Quilt

What you need:

- heavy paper cut into 9 squares (6 inches by 6 inches)
- crayons and markers
- fabric scraps
- tape

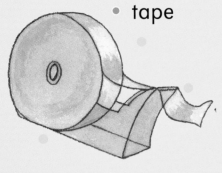

Directions:

1. Decorate each square using the crayons, markers, and fabric. Each square should be different. Use some of the q words from this book. You can make squares that have quarters on them, or a picture of a queen or a quail.

2. After your squares are finished, tape them together to make one large sheet. You should make three rows of three squares.

3. Display your Q quilt for everyone to see!

About the Author

Best-selling author Jane Belk Moncure has written over 300 books throughout her teaching and writing career. After earning a Master's degree in Early Childhood Education from Columbia University, she became one of the pioneers in that field. In 1956, she helped form the Virginia Association for Early Childhood Education, which established the first statewide standards for teachers of young children.

   Inspired by her work in the classroom, Mrs. Moncure's books have become standards in primary education, and her name is recognized across the country. Her success is reflected not only in her books' popularity with parents, children, and educators, but also by numerous awards, including the 1984 C. S. Lewis Gold Medal Award.

About the Illustrator

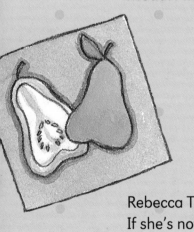

Rebecca Thornburgh lives in a pleasantly spooky old house in Philadelphia. If she's not at her drawing table, she's reading—or singing with her band, called Reckless Amateurs. Rebecca has one husband, two daughters, and two silly dogs.